ELEANOR ALLEN

Enter At
Your Peril

Illustrated by Nik Spender

Chapter One

All alone at the end of a lane, near David's new house, stood a tumbledown cottage. Timber-framed and lopsided, it had squinty little windows beneath a mouldy, straggly thatch that drooped over them, like half-closed lids. Behind was an overgrown orchard with gnarled and twisted trees. The cottage seemed deserted, yet full of ancient, scary secrets. David nicknamed it Creepy Cottage. It looked just the place for a spooky adventure – if he dared!

"I think I'll go down the lane and investigate Creepy Cottage," he told his mum, the day after they'd moved in.

Mum was surrounded by packing cases. She'd just told him to get out from under her feet, but now she didn't look too pleased.

"No you won't," she said. "It isn't empty. There's an old lady living there. And she hates to be disturbed. You're to stay away." She reached for her purse. "Why don't you go to the village shop and buy some crisps?"

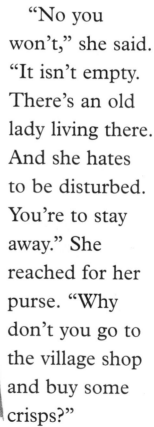

David bought the crisps. But when he walked home, he took the long way round. He went over a stile and across a field and back up the lane that led past Creepy Cottage.

Chapter Two

David stopped and stared at Creepy
Cottage over the garden gate. Even close
up, it had an empty and abandoned look.
Could somebody really be living there?

"Hey – you! Boy!"

David jumped with shock and guilt,
for the old lady herself had suddenly
appeared – out of nowhere, it seemed. She
was hovering on the pathway, right in
front of him, wearing a black coat and hat.
Her face was screwed up with anxiety.

"M-me?"

"Yes – *you*!"

She looked David up and down with a piercing stare. "You'll do!" she said.

"D-do?" he stammered in surprise. He'd been expecting a telling off.

"To feed my cat. I have to go away and there's nobody else to do it. His name's Tiger Tom." She creaked open the garden gate. "Come and meet him."

David backed away. "I-I have to get home," he muttered.

There was something about this old lady
that was even spookier than her cottage.
It was causing his knees to tremble. He
wondered what it was. It wasn't just the
blackness of her clothes, nor the deathly,
almost transparent paleness of her
wrinkled face... nor even the faint scent
that hung about her that reminded him
of old rose petals.

"Only take a minute," she said. "Look, there's Tiger Tom."

On the path had appeared a cat with ginger stripes.

"He's nineteen years old," the old lady said, her voice turning soft and proud.

Tiger Tom was still big-framed, but his flesh had shrunk away, leaving rolls of riffy-looking fur. There was a bald patch on his head and his eyes had a hazy look, as though he couldn't see too well. Bad case of the pongs too, David noticed.

"There's nobody else to feed him," the old lady repeated. "You must do it." She fixed David with a powerful stare. "He'll starve to death, otherwise."

David's eyes widened in alarm. Her words sent an icy chill through him. She

was making him responsible for keeping the cat alive. If he didn't feed it, it would die. And it would be all his fault. He slid his eyes from left to right, wanting to escape. But the old lady's stare seemed to pin him down as if she had cast a spell on him. "You wouldn't

leave a poor old cat to *starve to death*,
would you?"

David shook his head. "N-no," he gasped.
"I l-like cats."

The old lady nodded. "I could see that.
So come with me and I'll show you where
I keep his food."

David swallowed. He didn't want to
go inside Creepy Cottage. And he didn't
want to be landed with the responsibility
for an old mog that looked about to
breathe its last.

"Come on!" the old lady urged. "Don't dally around. I haven't got very long."

David's insides squirmed like a can of worms as he trailed after the old lady and her cat up the garden path.

Chapter Three

Cat dishes, food supply, cleaning stuff...
David glanced furtively around the
kitchen. Everything was very old and
worn. And there was a smell, of earthy
vegetables and washing-up and cups of tea
and plates of stew. It reminded him of the
past. Not the dead past, like in a museum.
In Creepy Cottage the past seemed
somehow still part of the present.

Tiger Tom stalked up to his dishes and sat beside them, swishing his ratty tail. He had a thin, ravenous look and he blinked at David impatiently.

"You can feed him now. Show me you can use the tin-opener."

David could feel the old lady hovering behind, checking he was doing it right. His hands shook as he opened up the can of meat and forked it out.

Tiger Tom pounced on the food and wolfed the lot.

The old lady nodded, satisfied.

"Six on the dot he likes his dinner," she said. "Make sure he's here when you put it out. He won't touch it if it's not fresh from the tin. Fussy in his old age, see?

"And mind that door to the hallway stays ajar. He has the run of the house."

Then she handed David a key.

How flickeringly dim and transparently pale the old lady looked, he thought. Like a lightbulb on the blink.

Hastily he pocketed the key and stepped outside. Then he stopped. He wondered if Tiger Tom should be given milk. He turned and looked inside again. But the kitchen was empty, apart from Tiger Tom. The old lady had gone, just as swiftly and as silently as she had first appeared.

David glanced across at the partly-open door that led deeper into the cottage. A spooky, scalp-prickling thought had dawned on him.

It wasn't just an elderly cat he was taking on. It was Creepy Cottage too. With its scary feel and its ancient secrets, and maybe even its ancient ghosts...

Chapter Four

No cat. David felt angry. The first couple of days, when he had sneaked away to feed him, Tiger Tom had been waiting by the door.

Nearly half past six. It was his mum's fault. Dragging him round the supermarket, making him late.

Cats know the time.

When was the old lady coming back? He realized she hadn't said. His mum would be getting suspicious if he kept on slipping out like this.

"Tiger! Tiger! Puss, puss, puss!"

David sighed and flipped the key impatiently. He stared towards the orchard. It was turning dark and a breeze had got up. Inside his warm anorak, David shivered.

He strode a metre or two into the
orchard and stopped. The place was alive
with hovering insects and darting bats.
"Tiger! Tiger!"
No response.

David groaned. He puffed angrily to hide
his mounting panic as he turned to face
the cottage door.

He pushed the door as wide open as he could. Then he stood very still, listening for sounds. Silence. Complete and utter silence. Not even a rafter creaked. Too much horrible silence, he thought.

David used his anger to break the silence. He grabbed a tin of cat food and rattled a fork hard against it. He shouted at the top of his voice.

"Tiger! Tiger!"

The name echoed back to him. Then the silence returned.

Drat the cat! What if he'd got shut in somewhere and couldn't get out?

David stared across the shadowy kitchen at the partly-open door that led into the hall. He felt full of dread at the thought of going through it. It's impossible to see who, or what's, behind a door that's partly open. But there's always the feeling that whatever it is could be watching you, through the crack.

David frowned. If he narrowed his eyes, he could imagine that the door had moved.

He grabbed the tin and started to open it with trembling hands. He would fill the dish full to the brim. Then he would scarper and never set foot in Creepy Cottage, ever again.

"Make sure he's there when you put it out. He won't eat it if it's not fresh. Don't want him to *starve to death*!"

David spun around. His hair had shot on end. He could have sworn the old lady had stealthily returned. That she was standing right behind him, reminding him of his duty. There was nobody there. Just a flicker of movement that must have been a shadow, caught from the corner of his eye. Yet among the kitchen smells, he thought he could detect the eerie scent of old rose petals.

A strangled sound came from his throat. He threw down the tin-opener guiltily. He knew he mustn't leave until the cat was found.

David faced the inner door and fought his dread. He creaked it open wide.

"Tiger!"

Chapter Five

There was an ordinary hallway, narrow and dark. He stepped inside.

Through an open door on the left he saw a little dining-room. It smelt musty and damp from years of under-use. There was no sign of Tiger Tom in there.

On the right was a sitting-room. It had a modern telly and a lived-in feel. Still no cat.

But David's courage began to mount.

Suddenly he felt determined to cover every inch. Throw wide open all the doors of Creepy Cottage. Make his presence felt. He clenched his fists and stamped his feet down hard as he climbed the stairs.

"Tiger!"

He flung wide the first door, at the back. A little bathroom, pink in colour, smelling of stale water and scented soap. He flung wide a second door. A bedroom, shabbily neat. He banged open a third door, at the front, and strode inside.

Another bedroom. Full of shadows and heavy, old-fashioned furniture. Across its little window drooped the thatch, tapping like ghostly fingers in the evening breeze.

The bedroom was full of silence. Silence so strong it seemed to wrap itself round him like a mist and fix him to the spot.

David ran his tongue across his lips. He suddenly felt afraid to move. Even to breathe. A clammy chill came over him and his flesh began to creep.

He squinted sideways, into the shadows.

Then he gasped. A coffin was lying there.

He stared at it. He blinked. He told himself it couldn't be real; that his eyes and the shadows were playing tricks.

But it was real. Real and shiny. Gleamingly new!

And he just *knew* there was a body in it.

A scream tore out of David's throat. He turned and ran. He plunged down the stairs, along the hallway and out of the kitchen door and down the path and out of the gate and away up the lane.

Chapter Six

David was half-way up the lane before he stopped.

He crouched down on the verge and clasped his head in his hands. His heart was thumping and his chest felt sore. He was trembling all over and his thoughts were knotted up.

What was he going to *do*?

Forget what he'd seen? Never go near Creepy Cottage ever again? *Yes!*

Something hard and sharp was digging into his thigh. He put his hand in his pocket and pulled out the key to Creepy Cottage.

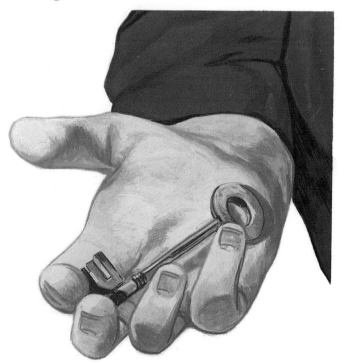

Throw the key away! he thought with a thudding heart. Pretend you never went there.

No! His heart had missed a beat. For there was something else. There was Tiger Tom.

"Too old to fend for himself. You wouldn't let a poor beast *starve to death*..."

It was the old woman's voice again, echoing in his ears.

David jerked his head around. Behind the hedge a tree was tossing troubled branches against the sky. Their dark shadows moved across his face. David was sure that for a second or two, behind his back, the shadows had darkened and lengthened and taken on the old woman's shape. But now there was no one there.

David heard a sob that came from him. He knew he couldn't leave the cat.

He scrambled to his feet and stumbled back along the narrow lane.

"Tiger!" he called in a strangled voice.

"Tiger!" he yelled in despair. He kicked in frustration at the garden gate, as the windows of Creepy Cottage winked down at him evilly through the gathering dusk.

"Don't make me go inside!" he
groaned. He closed his eyes and pleaded,
"Please don't make me go inside again!"

When he opened his eyes, a pale cat-
shape had appeared noiselessly on the
garden path. "Tiger! Oh Tiger!"

He pushed open the gate. "Here boy,
here! Puss, puss puss!"

On slow, stiff legs the old cat sidled up.

David reached out and grabbed him.
Tiger struggled indignantly, but David
was desperate and held on tight.

Clutching the bony bundle of wriggling,
protesting fur, he ran back up the lane
towards his house. Away from Creepy
Cottage.

Chapter Seven

"Good grief! What's that you've got?"

"It needs feeding," David gasped. He placed Tiger Tom gently on the kitchen floor.

"I know that cat," said David's mum. "It belonged to the old lady down the lane. I thought I told you to stay away from there!"

David ran a grubby hand sheepishly across his brow. "Have we any meat or fish?" he asked. "He's a very hungry cat."

David's mother eyed Tiger Tom. "Poor beast, he's probably starving! I don't expect anybody thought to feed him." She looked up. "It's very sad, David. The old lady's died. They were talking about it in the village shop. They brought her back in her coffin today, ready for the funeral tomorrow. She died five days ago, so that cat's lucky it's still alive."

David stared at his mother. His face was white beneath the streaks of dirt and his eyes had a wild and glassy look.

"W-when did the old lady die?" he whispered.

"Five days ago. The day before we moved in," she said.

"*Before* we moved in?'

"That's what I said. Are you OK? You've turned a funny colour..."

David nodded, but he sank down on to a kitchen chair. If the old lady had died the day before they moved in, there was no way he could have spoken to her the day *after*...

And yet he knew he had.

The truth shivered over him, like a ripple of cold air. He had seen a ghost.

He looked down at Tiger Tom. The old lady had loved the cat so much, she had come back from the dead to make sure he was fed.

Tiger Tom gave David a sly and knowing look and swished his ratty tail.

"There's a tin of pilchards in the cupboard," said David's mum. "I think you should be the one to feed him, David. It looks like somehow you've acquired a cat..."